ALLEN COUNTY PUBLIC LIBRARY

3 1833 01656 6041

P9-AGS-431

jE

Curious George goes to a
costume party

Curious George®
GOES TO A COSTUME PARTY

Adapted from the Curious George film series
edited by Margret Rey and Alan J. Shalleck

1 9 8 6
Houghton Mifflin Company Boston

Allen County Public Library
Ft. Wayne, Indiana

Library of Congress Cataloging-in-Publication Data

Curious George goes to a costume party.

"Adapted from the Curious George film series."
Summary: While trying to find a costume for a
party, George looks through Aunt Harriet's attic
and makes a huge mess.
[1. Parties—Fiction. 2. Costume—Fiction.
3. Monkeys—Fiction] I. Rey, Margret. II. Shalleck,
Alan J. III. Curious George goes to a costume party
(Motion picture) IV. Title.
PZ7.C9216   1986   [E]   86-7104
ISBN 0-395-42478-X   RNF
ISBN 0-395-42475-5   PAP

Copyright © 1986 by Houghton Mifflin Company and Curgeo Agencies, Inc.

All rights reserved. No part of this work may be
reproduced or transmitted in any form or by any means,
electronic or mechanical, including photocopying and
recording, or by any information storage or retrieval
system, except as may be expressly permitted by the 1976
Copyright Act or in writing from the publisher.
Requests for permission should be addressed in writing to
Houghton Mifflin Company, 2 Park Street,
Boston, Massachusetts 02108.

Printed in Japan

DNP   10   9   8   7   6   5   4   3   2   1

"George," said his friend,
"Aunt Harriet has just invited us to a party.
It sounds like fun — let's go!"

Aunt Harriet lived in an old house
with many rooms and a big attic.

"Hello, George," she said,
"I'm so glad you could come."

"Oh, but where is your costume?
I must have forgotten to tell your friend
that it's a costume party."

"But I know what you can do. You can make one up.
There are lots of things in the attic."

"George," said the man with the yellow hat,
"you can go up to the attic, but don't get
into trouble."

The attic was full of furniture,
a mirror, and boxes of old clothes.

George found a fireman's hat.

He tried it on, but it was too big for him.

Next, George tried on a sailor's suit.

This was too big, too.

The doorbell rang downstairs.
The guests were arriving.
George had to find a costume in a hurry!

On top of an old dresser was a big white sheet.
George was curious. Could he use that?

He reached up and pulled.

He pulled and pulled.

The sheet came off the dresser.
The old lamp came with it.

The lamp hit the floor
and broke into a hundred pieces.
And George got tangled in the sheet.

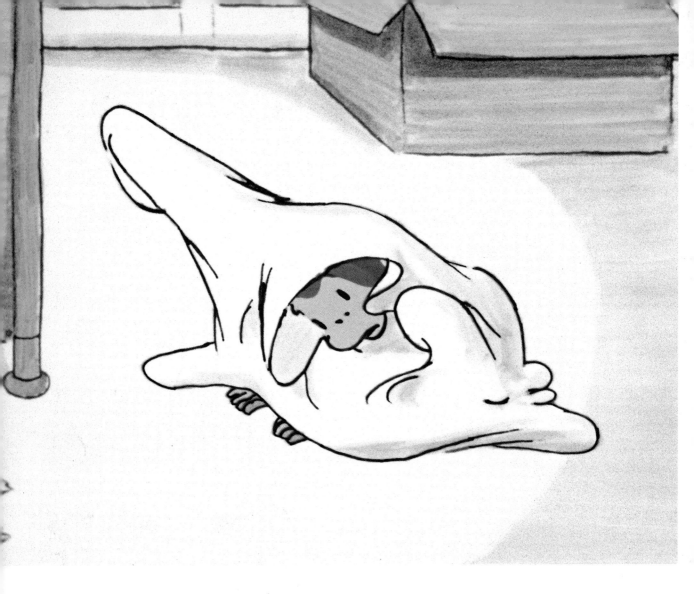

George tried to get out, but the more he tried,
the more tangled he became.

Then George heard voices coming from downstairs.

"Did you hear a crash upstairs?" someone asked.
"George, what are you doing up there?"
asked Aunt Harriet.

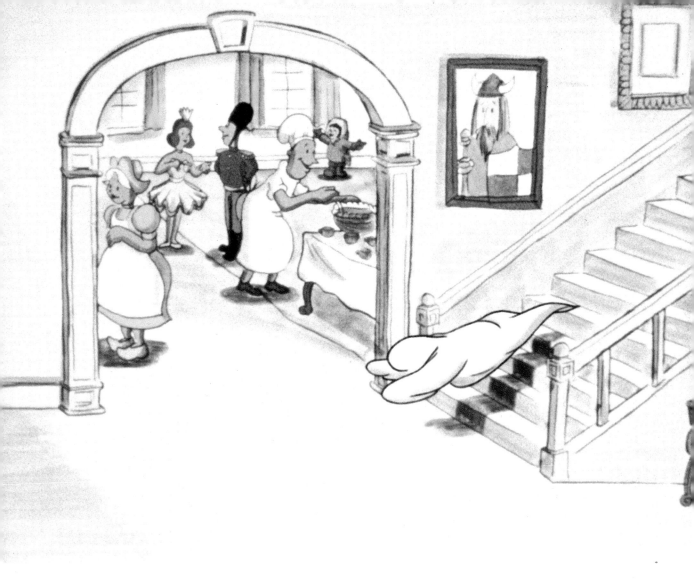

George was scared. He ran down the stairs,
still tangled in the sheet.

"Look!" someone shouted, "there goes a ghost!"

George ran faster.

Suddenly he tripped on the rug

and flew through the air.

George fell to the floor. "Stand back, everyone,"
said Aunt Harriet. "Let me take care of this."
Now George was trapped.

"George, it's you!" she said.
"You certainly gave us a scare dressed as a ghost!"

"George," said his friend, "did you break the lamp?"
"Don't mind the lamp," said Aunt Harriet.
"I never did like it."

"And," she added, "George made my party a big success."
"He should win first prize," someone shouted.

And George did.